Whodunit
Crime Mysteries

Hy Conrad

Illustrated by Tatiana Mai Wyss

D1516450

Sterling Publishing
New York

To Andy Breckman,
the man who gave me my chance in TV.

By the Same Author:

Almost Perfect Crimes

Almost Perfect Murders

Little Giant Book of Whodunits

Solve-It-Yourself Mysteries

Whodunit Crime Puzzles

Whodunit—You Decide!

Library of Congress Cataloging-in-Publication Data

Conrad, Hy.

Whodunit crime mysteries / Hy Conrad ; illustrated by Tatjana Mai Wyss.

   p.   cm.

Includes index.

Summary: The self-proclaimed great-great-grandson of Sherlock Holmes helps Sergeant Gunther Wilson solve a number of different cases.

Solutions for each mystery are given at the end of the book.

   ISBN 1-4027-0646-4

1. Mystery and detective stories.   I. Mai-Wyss, Tatjana, 1972- ill.

II. Title.

PZ7.C76473 Wh 2003

[Fic]--dc22

                                               2003015880

10 9 8 7 6 5 4 3 2 1

Published by Sterling Publishing Co., Inc.

387 Park Avenue South, New York, N.Y. 10016

© 2003 by Hy Conrad

Distributed in Canada by Sterling Publishing

c/o Canadian Manda Group, One Atlantic Avenue, Suite 105

Toronto, Ontario, Canada M6K 3E7

Distributed in Great Britain and Europe by Chris Lloyd at Orca Book Services, Stanley House, Fleets Lane, Poole,

BH1S 3AJ, England

Distributed in Australia by Capricorn Link (Australia) Pty. Ltd.

P.O. Box 704, Windsor, NSW 2756 Australia

Manufactured in the United States of America

All rights reserved

Sterling ISBN 1-4027-0646-4

Contents

Property Of
Wisconsin School for the Deaf

Introduction

FOR TEN YEARS, Sergeant Gunther Wilson had been a competent police detective, solving 42.5 percent of the major cases assigned to him, only slightly below the city average. The sergeant might have plodded along for another decade without making much of a name for himself, but then he had the greatest stroke of luck in his life. He ran into Sherman Holmes.

It all began one Halloween evening. The sergeant was at a murder scene in a small suburban home when the doorbell rang. At first, Wilson mistook the eccentric little man for a trick-or-treater. He was dressed in checkered pants, an old-fashioned frock coat and a deerstalker cap, with a mustache too perfectly trimmed to be real.

"I'm sorry, son," said Wilson. "No candy tonight. Who are you supposed to be, Sherlock Holmes?"

"Sherman Holmes," the odd figure said. His voice was too deep for a child's, and his natural southern drawl was tinged with a preposterous British accent. "Sherlock was my great-great-grandfather. If you let me have a look around, I might just be able to help you solve this case."

Wilson was about to send him away, but the little man

managed to squeeze under the sergeant's outstretched arms and into the house. That evening, Sherman Holmes solved his first case, although Sergeant Wilson wound up taking the credit. A week later, Sherman appeared at another murder scene, as if drawn there by a sixth sense. In a matter of months, the sergeant's record of solved cases skyrocketed.

Gunther Wilson had a sneaking suspicion that his new friend might be insane. He was certainly a fraud. After all, Sherlock Holmes had never really existed. But Sherman seemed harmless enough, and rich enough not to have to work. And, Wilson had to admit, he was the best crime-solver Capital City had ever seen.

The British Maid

IT WAS A SPRING AFTERNOON when Sherman Holmes's sixth sense led him down Main Street, and then left into an alley. Quickly, he realized he was approaching the rear of his favorite restaurant, The British Maid. "Good. As soon as I solve whatever bit of crime is waiting for me here, I'll make a reservation."

But when Sherman took in the scene in front of him, his heart fell. "No British Maid tonight," he thought. For there in the alley, directly behind the restaurant's service door, lay the body of Henry Bull, owner and chef. The knife was still in his stomach, imbedded up to its hilt and surrounded by a wet patch of crimson.

Three men stood over the deceased. Sherman knew them all. "Afternoon, my good fellows."

"Mr. Holmes," they said in near-unison.

"I told you he'd show up," said one of them to the others. "He's famous for turning up at murder scenes."

Sherman nodded. "Did anyone touch the body?"

"No," said Garth, the headwaiter. "We were just coming to work. We all got here within a minute of each other and this is what we found. It looks like a mugging to me."

"I called the police on my cell phone," said Hugo, the prep chef. "They should be here any minute."

Sherman bent down to examine the body. "Did that knife come from the restaurant kitchen?"

"Why, yes," said the third man, bending over to see. Joshua was the bread and pastry chef—best in the city, in Sherman's opinion. "All our knives have those identical black handles."

"So, Henry Bull's assailant must have been in the kitchen before the attack."

"It looks that way," said Hugo. "I check the equipment every night before leaving. Last night that short paring knife was in the rack with the others. Whoever killed the boss must have been inside the restaurant today."

Garth frowned. "Or maybe Henry was inside and heard a noise out here. Maybe he grabbed a knife, came

outside and caught a burglar trying to break in."

Sherman pulled a magnifying glass from his pocket and approached the kitchen door. He saw no signs of forced entry and no pick marks around the lock. "Did all of you get along with Mr. Bull?"

The three men exchanged glances. "You're asking if one of us had a reason to kill him," said Joshua. "Maybe one of us did."

"Josh!" Garth seemed upset by the chef's lack of discretion. "Mr. Holmes, you have to understand. Restaurants all have a little thievery. Steaks disappear from the freezer; friends get free drinks at the bar. An owner expects that. But Henry suspected some major stealing—grand larceny, according to him. Several employees have keys to The British Maid, including each of us. Henry thought this thief might be coming in early and doctoring the books to cover up his crime."

"That's probably what happened," said Joshua. "Henry caught the thief in the act. They argued and fought and probably continued the fight out here." He paused as the sound of sirens grew in the distance.

"Yes," said Sherman. "I suppose you're right." He was no longer worried about the crime. That part had been easy. What he was worried about now were his future dinners. Would The British Maid be able to survive without its owner—and without one of its key employees? He certainly hoped so.

Who killed Henry Bull?
What pointed Sherman to the killer?

Solution on page 79.

A Country Crime

"**T**HIS IS WHY I'M A CITY BOY," Sergeant Wilson said peevishly as he started picking hundreds of burrs off his pant legs. He and Sherman had just walked across an unplowed, bramble-choked field to arrive at the murder scene, the grassy bank of a river that separated two neighboring farms.

"I suppose we could have driven here," Sherman said, ignoring his own burrs. "Like these other people." He was looking at two vehicles, a pickup truck and a farm tractor, both parked on the grass just yards from the body.

"There's enough contamination of the crime scene without us adding to it," Wilson said. "Besides, you needed the exercise."

The victim, a middle-aged man in overalls, might have been napping under the shade of the weeping willow, except for the telltale pool of red that had seeped into the riverbank. A bloody tire iron lay a few feet from his mangled head.

"That's Earl, my brother," said a similar-looking man in overalls. The man introduced himself as Billy Bob

Lowry. Billy Bob and the deceased had run the farm and shared the rambling farmhouse with their younger sister, Glenda. Billy Bob and Glenda both stood on the grassy bank along with Amos Kinkaid, their neighbor from the farm across the river.

"When did you last see your brother alive?" asked the sergeant.

"I was in the barn on the far side of the house." Billy Bob pointed past the unplowed acreage in front of them to the distant farmhouse. Sherman could see Sergeant Wilson's car in the front drive and the top of a red barn behind it. "All morning I was working on the tractor," added Billy Bob. "About nine a.m. I looked out and saw Earl getting into his pickup and driving off. There was someone in the passenger seat, but I couldn't see who."

"Man or woman?"

"Don't know. I just saw the silhouette of a head above the seat."

"As far as I know, we didn't have any guests." Glenda

spoke softly and rubbed her hands up and down the neat, black surface of her skirt. "I was putting up preserves this morning when I ran out of jars. I needed to drive into town. I saw the pickup and walked over here to get it. That's when I found Earl, dead like this."

Wilson glanced inside the truck at the passenger seat. "I'll have forensics vacuum it, although I don't hold out much hope." He turned to Amos, the neighbor. "How did you happen upon the scene?"

Amos pointed to his own pickup on the far side of the river. "I was driving along the river path when I heard Glenda calling for help. I stopped and walked across."

Sherman noticed that the man's trousers were wet from the hips down.

"That's right," said Billy Bob with a nod. "I drove up in the tractor at about the same time Amos got here. We used my cell phone to call the police. No one's moved from this spot until you guys arrived."

Wilson took his friend aside. "We'll have to question them separately. Maybe we'll come up with a motive."

"I don't know about motives," Sherman whispered back. "But I know which suspect is lying."

Whom does Sherman suspect?
What did the suspect lie about?

Solution on page 80.

The Halloween Devil

THE RAIN HAD ENDED in the afternoon, leaving a chilly but clear evening for the trick-or-treaters. As usual, Sherman donned his full Sherlock Holmes regalia and milled among the costumed youngsters on the street. Sherman was at his very happiest on Halloween.

It was growing late and he was just passing a vacant lot when he heard a moan. Nothing moved in the darkened lot, but the observant little man noticed a single set of footprints in the mud. "Hello!" he called out and was answered with another moan.

Sherman followed the prints into the lot, around the

trash barrels and trees, until he found a young man collapsed in a corner. He'd been stabbed in the stomach. The wounds were more than superficial. He needed medical attention.

"Some guy in a devil mask," he groaned. "Chased me with a knife, for no reason. I ran in here, but I fell and he got me." The wound was still bleeding. "He must've thought I was dead."

"You'll be all right," Sherman promised. "I'm going for help."

Sirens were approaching. As Sherman emerged from the lot, he saw an ambulance and a patrol car a block down the street. Waddling at his top speed, he flagged down the

ambulance and told the paramedics the situation.

"Go get the guy in the lot," a familiar voice shouted from the depths of another nearby alley. "You can't help this one. She's dead."

The ambulance driver and crew did as they were told, leaving Sherman to push his way through the gathering crowd. Sergeant Gunther Wilson, the owner of the voice, stood over the body of a young woman in an angel costume.

"Stabbed?" Sherman asked.

"Hi." Wilson's voice lacked its usual gruffness. "Yeah, stabbed in the chest and stomach. Looks like she put up a fight before she died."

Sherman informed Wilson about the other attack.

"That fits," Wilson said. "People were mentioning some strange-acting guy in a devil costume."

The sergeant was interrupted by his two-way radio.

"The guy in the lot's going to make it," he told Sherman. "My boys found a devil costume nearby. Also a mask and a knife. Let's hope this was his last victim."

Wilson told a patrolman to tape off the site. "And check the crowd. I want to see any adult male not with kids and not wearing a costume."

The patrolman and his partner returned a few minutes later with two men fitting that rather broad description. The first was a slight man, apparently in his thirties. A closer glance at the lines around the eyes and his jet-black toupee told Sherman that he was at least ten years older. He was dressed in a black sweatshirt, black jeans, and a pair of slippers.

"What were you doing here?" Wilson asked.

"I live here," the man said, pointing to a red brick house. The windows were dark and the house looked empty. "I don't hand out candy. I was in my bedroom watching TV and ignoring the doorbell. When I heard the sirens, I came out. Is that a crime?"

"No, sir," Wilson replied, turning to the second suspect, a man in his early twenties with a scraggly goatee and disheveled hair.

"My car broke down over on the next block," he answered without having to be asked. "I was just walking up to some house to use their phone when your jack-booted buddy grabbed me."

The sergeant took Sherman aside. "At least we have a surviving witness, but he may not be much help if the attacker was wearing a mask."

"Well, if our survivor can't identify him, I can."

"I was hoping you'd say that," Wilson said with a grin.

Who was the masked attacker?
What clue gave him away?

Solution on page 80.

Murder on Vacation

SINCE SHERMAN DIDN'T HAVE A JOB, he didn't much bother with vacations. But this summer, the amateur detective decided to leave the crime of Capital City in the hands of the police and drove himself to the seaside resort of Brighton, where he traded in his tweed frock coat for a tweed bathing suit.

He had just checked into his hotel room and was enjoying the ocean view from his balcony when he noticed a chip broken out of the top edge of the stone railing. A second later, he saw a sliver of yellow police tape caught in the balcony door. "What happened here?" he asked the bellhop. The boy put down the luggage and smiled. "We had a murder," he said, still excited by the recent event. "On this exact balcony. Unsolved—so far."

Sherman tipped the boy, brought him a soft drink from the mini-bar, then sat him down and demanded a full accounting.

Mary McDill, a middle-aged widow, had stayed here for two weeks and, during that time, fell madly in love with Sonny Arbor, the resort's tennis pro.

"They were together all the time," the bellhop

confided, "until towards the end. That's when he dumped her for another guest, one with more money, so they say. Ms. McDill became unbalanced and caused a few scenes. So one day, Sonny was having lunch with Ms. Rubinski; that's the other woman. Ms. McDill came up to their table and started yelling, saying how she knew things, how she was going to the police and ruin Sonny's life the way he ruined hers."

That afternoon Mary McDill sent Sonny a threatening note, telling him to come to her room at six p.m. At a few minutes after six, a maid knocked on Ms. McDill's door, hoping to turn down the bed and leave a mint. She heard shouts coming from inside. A woman's voice was screaming, "No, Sonny, no! Don't shoot!" Then there was a single gunshot.

The frightened maid ran off. When she returned with Security, they found Mary McDill's body alone on the balcony, a bullet hole in her head.

"Why is the case unsolved?" asked Sherman. "It seems pretty clear..."

"Sonny Arbor had an alibi," the bellhop chuckled. "At

six p.m., he was stuck in traffic on the coast road. People from the hotel recognized him in his convertible."

Sherman was intrigued. "Tell me about the physical evidence."

The victim, he learned, had been shot from about a foot away and the gun thrown off the balcony and into the sea. The killer then tied a weight around the gun butt with a six-foot length of rope. It was recovered the next morning in the water under the balcony.

"The only other piece of evidence was a handkerchief with bits of gunpowder on it. Guess where they found it." Sherman didn't even try.

"On that balcony down there." The bellhop pointed to a balcony one floor down and one room over. "That was Sonya Rubinski's room."

"The other woman." Sherman appreciated the coincidence. "And what's her alibi?"

"A maid was working on that floor. A few seconds after the shot, Ms. Rubinski came out of her room and asked her what the noise was."

"I see." Sherman stared down at the waves lapping the pylons that supported this end of the hotel.

"A stumper, huh?" the bellhop said. "The victim calls out a name. Could be Sonny or maybe Sonya. Yet both suspects have alibis."

"Not a stumper," Sherman said with a happy sigh. "Any student of my great-great grandfather's work would know the answer."

Who killed Mary McDill?
How was the crime committed?

Solution on page 81.

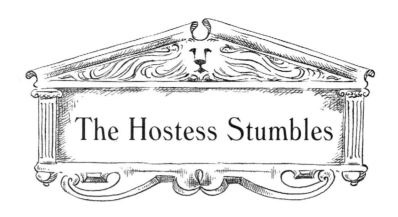

The Hostess Stumbles

SHERMAN WAS A MORNING PERSON, even on weekend trips. On this particular Sunday, he had done his morning exercises, shaved and showered, and then raided his hostess's kitchen, all before eight a.m. He opened a new gallon of milk, poured himself a full glass, and retired to the dining room. He was just taking a long swallow when two other guests stumbled down the stairs.

"Morning," yawned Lucas Mint. "How did you sleep?"

"Like a log," Sherman answered. Their hostess, Alice Darden, was known for her hospitality. The middle-aged widow had made her guests feel perfectly at home in the cozy country house.

"This is a nice change," said Delia White, the second late riser. "The five of us usually meet just once a month, and then it's all business."

The four guests and their hostess were the sole members of an investment club and, although Sherman knew nothing about finances, he enjoyed the camaraderie and the profits.

"I think this is more than a social get-together," Lucas

said, lowering his voice. "Did anyone else notice Alice's behavior?"

Just then the fourth guest wandered into the dining room, cradling a cup of coffee. "I noticed," he whispered.

Bernie Grouper, a normally cheerful young man, was looking uncharacteristically worried. "Alice let fly with some cryptic comments at our last meeting."

"Yes," Sherman agreed. "She did make a few jokes about shady bookkeeping, but I thought she was just railing against the Federal Reserve."

Delia picked a piece of lint off her fluffy guest bathrobe. "Well, all of us do a portion of the bookkeeping, except Sherman, of course, who's hopeless in that area."

"I wonder if Delia was serious," said Lucas, "and if she has any proof—or just suspicions."

Their musings were interrupted by a voice from the kitchen: "Oh, drat!" A few seconds later, Alice walked into the dining room. "Morning, everyone. I'll be back in

a minute." Then she threw Sherman a decidedly hostile look, grabbed her car keys from a bowl and headed out the front door.

"What was that about?" Delia said with a muffled giggle.

Before anyone could speculate, there came the sound of cracking wood, followed by a crash. The guests raced to the front door and threw it open.

Alice's house was set on a bluff. Poised over a ravine stood a footbridge connecting the house to the parking area by the road. Half the bridge was no longer there. The center section had collapsed under Alice's weight, sending her tumbling onto the river rocks below.

"She's alive," Lucas said. Lucas and Bernie skidded down the sides of the ravine, while Delia hurried back inside to call for help.

Sherman took his time. He watched his friends trying to help the injured woman, then turned his attention to the edges of wood by the break. Someone had sawn through them, he noticed, ensuring that the bridge would collapse. He didn't want to suspect one of his friends of attempted murder, but the evidence was unmistakable.

Back in the kitchen, Sherman opened the refrigerator, found what he was looking for—or rather found that what he was looking for was missing—then checked the wastebasket under the counter. "Yes," Sherman muttered. "We may just have a shady bookkeeper in our midst. And a prospective killer."

Whom does Sherman suspect?
What was in the wastebasket?

Solution on page 82.

Found Money

ONCE A WEEK, Sherman had lunch at the Baskerville, a delicatessen not far from his home. On this afternoon, a sunny Wednesday in June, he walked up to the counter and ordered his usual ham and Swiss sandwich. As he paid, he couldn't help noticing that Irene, the cashier, seemed distracted.

"Something's afoot," he muttered, and wasn't at all surprised two minutes later when Gunther Wilson strolled through the door. Sherman watched as the police sergeant spoke privately with Irene, their heads bent together over the cash register. Eventually Wilson turned, saw his old friend and rolled his eyes, a typical greeting that Sherman never took offense at.

"I shouldn't be annoyed to find you at another crime scene." Wilson sat down at Sherman's table. "So? You want to make yourself useful?"

The pudgy detective saw the twenty-dollar bill in Wilson's hand. "A counterfeiting case?"

"Wrong," Wilson said with obvious pleasure. "Stolen money. I suppose it was stolen."

"You suppose?"

"It happened Thursday." Wilson leaned across and whispered. "An armored truck was making pick-ups at some branch banks. As they were loading the bags, one of the guards accidentally left a bag of bills on the rear bumper. They drove off and didn't notice a thing until the next stop. They counted the bags in the truck and figured out what must have happened. Somewhere on York Boulevard, the bag must have fallen onto the road. They went back to look for it..."

"But it was gone," Sherman interrupted. "Do you believe the guards' story?"

"I do," said Wilson. "These guys could lose their jobs and their pensions, which are worth more than a bag of money. I'm betting some average guy found it on the road and his greed overcame his civic responsibility."

"That still makes it stealing."

"I know. Luckily, the bills were numbered sequentially. We got a list out to local merchants. Irene here matched the number on this twenty and phoned it in. The person who passed the bill had to be one of her last three customers—not including you, of course."

Sherman glanced at the three lone diners, each at a separate table. "Excuse me," he told Wilson, then crossed to the nearest diner and, in his friendliest manner, engaged her in conversation.

"I was just transferred to this area," the young woman confided, glad to have someone to talk to. "I'm hunting for a house, but everything is so expensive."

"There are some nice houses on York Boulevard," Sherman said.

"I checked that neighborhood last week. I didn't notice any 'For Sale' signs."

Sherman gave the woman the name of an ace real estate agent, then moved on to the next table. A muscular young man in a sweat-stained tracksuit was finishing a tuna sandwich.

"I got a prize fight next week," he bragged, "and I'm on a strict routine, every day without fail. One day the gym; next day sparring; the next road work, like today; then back to the gym."

"Do you ever jog along York Boulevard?"

The boxer thought for a moment. "Yeah, I was running there last Wednesday. That was my birthday. A nice road, not much traffic."

The last diner was dressed in cycling gear, with a helmet hooked over an empty chair back. "Sure, I ride on York Boulevard," he told Sherman. "It's part of my daily loop. Fifteen miles, then a veggie burger here, and five more miles around the reservoir. You should try a little exercise."

"Exercise." Sherman shuddered as he walked back to Wilson and his lunch. "I get all the exercise I need bringing in the bad guys."

Whom does Sherman suspect?
What evidence points to the thief?

Solution on page 83.

Crime in Record Time

SHERMAN TOSSED AND TURNED, unable to sleep. Part of the reason might have been the strange environment. He was spending the weekend in the country with Howard and Joey Myers, two bachelor brothers who owned a local restaurant.

Part of the reason might have been the lumpy sofa bed in the living room that Sherman was forced to sleep on. Or maybe it was the early bedtime. A passing storm had knocked out the electricity, and after a few candlelit hands of gin, everyone gave up and headed off to bed.

But Sherman was convinced it was his sixth sense that was keeping him up. The only other guest was Howard's fiancee, Eliza, who'd spent the day flirting with Joey, the younger, more attractive brother. Given the Myers family temper, it was a surefire recipe for disaster.

Sherman was jolted awake when the electricity returned. The TV began to blare and a digital clock on the end table flashed back to life. He fumbled for the remote and punched off the TV. A second later he saw a shadow tiptoeing across the living room.

"What time is it?" Sherman mumbled.

The shadow was Joey, and he checked his watch. "It's

11:30. Go to sleep. I'm driving back to the city. It's too uncomfortable with Eliza acting the way she is."

"Good idea," Sherman agreed. From the discomfort of the sofa bed, he watched as Joey went out the front screen door, got into his car and drove down the long winding driveway.

Sherman must have finally dozed off, for the next thing he knew it was daylight and Howard's bedroom door was knocking into the sofa. "I'm going to need you to fold that up so I can get out," Howard said from behind the door.

Sherman did as he was told, getting out of bed, folding it up and lying about what a good night sleep he'd had.

The two men went into the kitchen to make coffee and chat. It was a few minutes later when they discovered that not only was Joey gone, but so was Eliza. Howard immediately suspected the worst.

"They've run off together," he snarled.

But that wasn't true. Eliza was still around. Her bludgeoned body lay on the railroad tracks that bordered the north side of the Myers property.

The county police responded to their emergency call. While Howard collapsed in the gazebo, stunned by the tragedy, Sherman explained as much as he could to the officer in charge. He was more than a little surprised when Gunther Wilson drove up.

"This isn't your jurisdiction," Sherman said as the two shook hands.

"I'm here as a friend," Wilson explained. "Sherman, you're a suspect."

"Me?" He was outraged at the thought.

"Yes, you. According to what you told the police, it can't be Howard."

"True," Sherman agreed. "He couldn't get out of his room last night, not without moving the sofa bed. The windows in his room are painted shut, so there's no other way out."

"And it can't be Joey."

"True. Eliza's body was on the tracks. And since she wasn't run over by the 11:45 night train, we know she was killed after 11:45, after Joey drove off alone. But maybe Joey drove to the tracks where Eliza was already waiting."

"No," Wilson said. "The storm left a nice patch of mud on the driveway, perfect for tire tracks. One car drove off the property, with no detours."

"Leaving me as the prime suspect," Sherman moaned.

Sherman and Wilson walked back into the house.

"Is that the correct time?" Sherman asked. He was pointing to the clock on the end table. "Is it eleven a.m. already?"

Wilson checked his watch. "A few minutes after eleven. Why?"

"I think I solved this crime in record time—so to speak."

Who killed Eliza?
How did the killer give himself an alibi?

Solution on page 83.

Wilson Wins One

"**Z**ACH ALBANS HAS THE WORST LUCK," Sherman sighed as Sergeant Wilson pulled into a parking space in front of the store. The sign on the roof proclaiming Albans Jewelers had just been installed this morning. The shop wasn't even open for business and it had already been robbed.

Zach Albans rushed out to greet them. "Sherman," he said, pumping his old friend's hand. "I thought changing locations would change my luck, but I guess not."

Albans escorted them inside. The officers who'd answered the call were examining the empty glass case while Albans' two employees stood around, looking helpless. The shop owner used to employ three people until last year when one had been arrested for robbery.

"How did it happen?" Sherman asked.

"We were setting up the display cases," Albans told his friend. "The space isn't ready; we don't even have a working bathroom. But our opening party is tonight, so we have to make do. At around noon, I went into the back office. Our front door was propped open—no air conditioning yet. I figured either Melanie or Ricky was in the front showroom watching things. Seems I was wrong. They'd both stepped out. That gave the thief enough time to see the rings, run into the store and grab all six of them. They're insured, of course, but only at wholesale value."

"I'll do my best," Sherman said and crossed over to Wilson who was shaking hands with Melanie, the manager.

"I had to go around the corner and feed the parking meter," she said, then glared accusingly at Ricky. "I told him to stay here. When I came back, the showroom was empty and the rings were gone. I ran into the back. Zach was on the phone. He hung up right away and we called the police."

Wilson thanked Melanie for her help, then ambled over to speak with Ricky Mayfield.

"I shouldn't have left the front door open," said the guilt-stricken employee. "But I didn't know if Melanie had her key with her or not. After Melanie left, I ran to the coffee shop next door to use their bathroom. Since I

wasn't a customer, I kind of sneaked in. I don't know if anyone saw me. Zach and Melanie were here when I got back, trying to figure out how much had been stolen."

"Sergeant Wilson? Can you come out here?"

The voice had come from the store's open courtyard located directly behind the showroom. An officer was standing by the pine tree in the middle of the shady yard. His hand was wet with pinesap, but there was a red felt bag in his hand and a smile on his face. "I reached inside a hole in the tree and found this bag wedged in a crevice."

Wilson took the sticky bag into the showroom and opened it. The rings were all there, safe and sound.

"What do you think?" whispered Wilson.

"Obviously an inside job," Sherman whispered back. "Zach could have taken them when the store was empty. The same with Melanie or Ricky. The thief wedged them inside the tree, knowing he or she could get them later. It's a bit too early to know which one."

Wilson grinned. "Too early for you, but I know."

Sherman tried to hide his shock. How could Wilson know and not him? What bit of information did the sergeant have that Sherman didn't? He was mortified.

And then he realized what must have happened.

Who stole the rings?
What evidence did Wilson have?

Solution on page 84.

Murder Works Weekends

WILSON AND HOLMES WERE ENJOYING a Saturday breakfast at the Baker Street Coffee Shop when the call came in. "Murder on a weekend?" Sergeant Wilson muttered between bites of his cheese omelet. "What's this world coming to?"

They arrived at the law offices of Wynn, Loose, and Draw to find Chester Wynn sprawled on his Oriental rug, his left temple a bloody mess. The usual group of three suspects stood in the reception area outside the victim's private office in the company of an officer.

"Why are you people working today?" Wilson barked.

A tall man in a polo shirt stepped forward. "An old client just filed a lawsuit against Chester for malpractice," he explained. "It could cost the firm millions. Of course, with Chester dead, we stand a much better chance of winning."

The tall man introduced himself—Kiefer Loose, the law firm's new senior partner. "We came in today to get a jumpstart on the suit."

The only woman of the group stepped forward. "We all arrived at about the same time," said Penelope Draw, a

middle-aged attorney with a no-nonsense attitude. "Chester went into his office and closed the door. I had documents to prepare for the meeting. I went back and forth between my office and the document center." She pointed to a cubicle outfitted with copy machines and supplies.

"I had just finished making copies for everyone and binding them when I heard Chester shouting. Then came a loud thud. I knocked on his door. The others were knocking on his two other doors. We all walked in and found him. Someone had hit him with that award from his desk. Lawyer of the Year. Funny, huh?"

Kiefer Loose didn't smile at the irony. "I was in my own office," he said, "right beside Chester's. Like Penelope said, we all heard the murder. My side door opens directly into Chester's office. I knocked and heard the others knocking."

The third suspect was a bulky young man. "Ben Tingly," he announced and shook the sergeant's hand. "Junior partner. There are no secretaries today, so I took it on myself to set up the conference room. As you can see, it's also next to Chester's office, on the other side, and has a connecting door. My story is the same. I heard Chester and what I suppose was the attack."

Sherman wandered around the office. He examined the pile of freshly bound background documents, then crossed to Keifer Loose's door. Inside, he could see a golf club and a water glass lying sideways on the rug. Strolling past the conference room door, he glanced in and saw four places set at the table, with water carafes, crystal tumblers, pens, and tablets at each place setting.

"What did you do after calling the police?" Sherman asked.

"Nothing," Ben replied. "We all came into the conference room and just sat down until your people arrived."

Kiefer Loose nodded and sighed. "Well, as long as we're here, we may as well have the meeting. Excuse us, sergeant." He grabbed the background documents from the top of the copy machine and passed out all three of them, one to each partner of the firm.

"Bunch of cold fish," Wilson muttered as they disappeared into the conference room. "I hope you got someone for me to arrest, Holmes. That'll wipe the smug off their faces."

Who killed Chester Wynn?
What clue implicates the killer?

Solution on page 85.

Door-To-Door Homicide

SERGEANT GUNTHER WILSON had been at the crime scene for over an hour when he finally heard the roar of the antique Bentley pulling up to the small suburban house. "It's about time," he yelled out the open front door.

As Sherman Holmes walked up the front path, he couldn't make out what Wilson was saying, but the growl in the sergeant's voice told him he'd been expected.

"Sorry," said Holmes in his best Alabama-English accent. "I was in the middle of a nap when the feeling woke me up. What do we have here, a murder?"

Wilson nodded toward a pool of blood near the rear corner of the living room. "Delia Waterford. Elderly widow. Body's already been removed. She was hit over the head with a marble statuette. From the missing money and jewelry, we're thinking a robbery."

"My aunt was too trusting," volunteered a young, attractive woman, the only civilian in the room. "She'd let in any salesman or bum off the street. I told her a million times."

"This is Nan Waterford, the victim's niece," said

Wilson. "She and a neighbor discovered the body."

Nan Waterford sighed. "Every Thursday I come and drive Aunt Delia around. I'm her only close relative, so it's up to me to be her chauffeur. I called from my cell phone just as I was pulling up, around two p.m. Her answering machine picked up, but that wasn't unusual. Auntie often screened her calls. Mr. Klinger, the next-door neighbor, had just come outside to water his flowers. Auntie didn't answer my knock. The door was unlocked and … Well, as soon as I saw her, I guess I screamed. Mr. Klinger came in and checked for a pulse while I dialed 911."

"Have you finished dusting for prints?" said Sergeant Wilson to no one in particular.

A forensics officer popped his head in from the kitchen. "Yeah, living room's done. No prints on the statuette, the water glass, the drawer knobs, answering machine and jewelry case. There were dozens, maybe hundreds of other prints in the room. Looks like she didn't dust too often."

Wilson crossed to the answering machine and pressed the blinking red button. "Aunt Delia." It was Nan Waterford's voice. "I'm pulling up in front. I hope you're

ready to go. I only have three hours today." A mechanical voice set the time at 1:57 p.m.

Sherman had wandered to the table by the front door and picked up a notepad. "Prescriptions. Doctor 2:30. Lawyer 3:30," he read aloud, then stopped and inspected the remaining surface of the table. "Were there other papers here?"

"Good guess," said Wilson. "Yes, we found a receipt for a magazine subscription company and a leaflet from the Wetlands Foundation. I sent some officers around the neighborhood..."

The sergeant was interrupted by the return of one of those officers.

"Sergeant Wilson?" He had in tow a short man hugging a large, cheap briefcase. "This is Doug Hilton. He was canvassing the area for Apex Subscription Service."

"Good job, officer." Wilson beamed and eased a hand onto Doug Hilton's shoulder. "Did you sell the owner of this house some magazines today?"

"Yeah," said Hilton, looking more than a little nervous. "She bought 12 subscriptions. Paid in cash. Terrific old lady. Afterwards, I finished this block and then went to a bar on Tower Street to celebrate."

"I found him in the bar," the officer said. "He was celebrating, all right."

Even Sherman could smell the alcohol. "What time were you here, Mr. Hilton?"

The salesman thought for a second. "Maybe one. Maybe later. I don't have a watch, so it's hard to say."

Wilson cleared his throat. "Mr. Hilton, that terrific old lady was robbed and murdered."

"Murdered? Oh, no."

This time the interruption came from a young, thin man with pimply skin and a clipboard, a college student from the look of him. He was standing in the doorway, in the company of another officer.

"I picked this guy up three blocks over," the officer told his sergeant. "He was just getting into his car."

Wilson gave the new arrival a cold smile. "Are you from the Wetlands Foundation? Did you knock on this door today?"

"Yes," the young man gulped. "The old lady signed my petition." He checked his clipboard. "Delia Waterford. She also made a contribution—a generous contribution. In cash. I wanted to write a receipt but she said it wasn't necessary."

"I see," Wilson said. "A frail, old lady opening her door to anyone and flashing lots of money. I'm surprised she lasted this long. What time were you here, Mr..."

"Abrams. Chuck Abrams. I canvassed this block after lunch. Sometime around one."

"I see." Wilson turned and grabbed Sherman by the elbow, pulling him away. "Well, they obviously weren't here at the same time. The earlier guy is in the clear, of course, but which one was earlier?"

Sherman just smiled one of those smiles that made Wilson want to commit his own murder, right then and there.

Who killed Delia Waterford?
What clue pointed Sherman to the Killer?

Solution on page 85.

What the Killer Forgot

DESPITE ALL THE PLEASURES OF CRIME-SOLVING, despite all the hours he spent with the police Sherman Holmes was never comfortable in police stations. So late one evening, when Sergeant Wilson suggested they meet at Precinct House #5, Sherman found himself pacing nervously in the station's vestibule, just outside the lobby, waiting for his friend to arrive.

"Mr. Holmes, hello! You waiting for the Sarge?" It was Officer Maloney, a beefy giant with a broad grin. "There are chairs inside, you know."

"That's hardly necessary. Wilson said he'd be here by 10:30."

"And what time is it now?"

How can people not wear watches? Sherman wondered, as he unpocketed his silver pocket watch. "10:26. Just a few more minutes."

"Is that an antique?" A second officer had just entered the station and immediately noticed Sherman's elaborate timepiece.

"Oh, hello, Officer Valdez." He held out the watch for inspection. "As a matter of fact, yes. It belonged to my great-great grandfather, Sherlock Holmes."

Valdez was a dark, weathered, rather serious-looking man who'd worked with Sherman on several cases. "Was that passed down in the family," he quipped, "or did you buy it in a pawn shop?"

Before Sherman could reply, a third policeman joined them. It was near the beginning of their shift. Pretty soon a dozen more officers would make their way into the vestibule, unlocking the door of the locker room and going inside.

"Officer Longo," said Sherman with a wave. He prided himself on knowing most of the boys in blue by name.

"Hey, Shermie," said the tall, friendly patrolman as he fiddled with his key chain. "You guys gonna stand here all night or are you coming to work?" And with that, he unlocked the door and sauntered in. Maloney and Valdez accompanied him into the warren of cubicles where they would change into their uniforms.

The amateur detective was once again left by himself, but only for a minute. The locked door opened and officers Valdez and Longo both poked out their heads. "Shermy?" asked Longo sheepishly. "Can you come in here?"

Sherman followed them into the locker room. There, lying by an open locker, was the body of Lieutenant Wheeler, a bloody nightstick lying inches from his fractured skull. Officer Maloney stood guard over the body, looking as stricken as the other two.

"We found him as soon as we walked in," Longo said with a shake of the head. "Body's still warm."

"I know we have to follow procedure," said Valdez. "But to have a cop murdered in the precinct house, and by another cop..."

"By another cop?" Sherman asked, stunned by the thought.

"Only cops have keys to the locker room," said Maloney. He pointed to a door marked exit. "There's an emergency exit but it only pushes out."

"And the only entrance is the one in the vestibule?"

"Right," said Longo. "So unless you can work your magic and tell us how an outsider could have gotten in here..."

Sherman had always dreamed of this moment, to be surrounded by police officers all pleading for his help. He

visually examined the half-dressed man. "Was he leaving work or arriving?"

"Leaving, I guess," said Longo. "The Lieutenant worked Internal Affairs, on the trail of dirty cops."

"Could he have been meeting an officer here?"

"It's possible," said Valdez. "Near the end of one shift, near the beginning of another."

"Did any of you speak with him recently?" Sherman asked. "What was he working on?"

Maloney shrugged. "This is my first shift since my vacation. I haven't seen Wheeler in weeks."

"I saw him yesterday," said Valdez. "He didn't say much, but I got the feeling he was close to breaking something big."

"He questioned me about a week ago," said Longo. The young man seemed uncomfortable. "He was looking into accusations of a cop taking payoffs from a gambling club."

"A cop on the night shift?" asked Sherman.

"Maybe that's who he was meeting," Valdez said, lowering his voice. "A dirty cop on the night shift who thought Wheeler was getting too close to the truth."

The locker room fell into a long silence. "Ah-hem," Maloney finally said, checking his watch. "The rest of the guys are gonna be coming in any second. What do you think we should do? Mr. Holmes?"

Sherman had a good idea, and the idea centered on one of the three officers in front of him.

Which cop does Sherman suspect?
What made him suspicious?

Solution on page 86.

Crime at
Criminy Woods

ONCE EVERY AUTUMN, Sherman Holmes went home to Alabama. There he would spend the better part of a week visiting his childhood friends and then, for another few days, go off by himself and rent a cabin in the woods. This was his annual attempt to forget crime and return to nature, although he did spend hours doing surveillance work on possums or trying to discover who or what murdered a particular squirrel.

It was on the last day of Sherman's latest trip that he found himself the victim of a robbery.

The time was early evening, and the rotund little detective was about to unwrap a sandwich when there was a knock on the cabin door. Without thinking twice, he

opened it and was suddenly facing a masked man in a base-ball cap, medium height, medium build, aiming a gun at his head. "Give me your wallet," whispered the robber.

For a man who had helped incarcerate dozens of thieves and killers, Sherman did not react well. "Please don't hurt me," he whispered back and immediately reached over to the nearby dresser where his wallet lay open and bulging.

Two minutes later, he was tied to a chair, a gag in his mouth, with all his valuables stolen from the small single-room cabin.

Sherman was just working the gag loose from his mouth when there came another knock. "Mr. Holmes? Are you okay? Mr. Holmes?" The door opened and Sherman was relieved to see Frank Lower, the young manager of Criminy Woods Rental Cabins.

"He got you, too," Frank said and ran to untie Sherman from the chair.

Frank, it seems, had been alone in his office/cabin when he was attacked by the same masked robber. The only difference was that Frank had put up a struggle and had been knocked unconscious for his effort.

"He got the cash box." Frank said, nursing a bump on the back of his skull. "And he took my wallet and my ring."

"Let's check the other cabins," Sherman said as he hurried out the door.

From the cars in the parking area, they could see that only two other cabins were currently occupied. Their first stop was the cabin right beside Sherman's. Like the others, it was a one-room structure plus a bathroom, with three tiny windows and a single door. The door was partially open and Sherman didn't bother to knock.

"Hello? Are you all right?"

Lola and Jim Grimm, a middle-aged couple, were on the floor in the middle of the room, Lola tied to a chair and gagged, and Jim recovering from a blow to the head. "He knocked Jim out with his gun," said Lola when Frank removed the gag. "Then he tied me up and ransacked the room." Sherman could see the turned-out drawers and the opened suitcases on the bed.

The last cabin was perhaps fifty yards away, by the riverbank. The other three victims stood behind Sherman as he turned the knob and pushed the door. It opened a few inches before hitting something. That something moaned.

"Mr. Boatman?" Sherman called through the crack.

"Help," a disoriented voice replied. "I've been mugged."

Jonas Boatman soon recovered enough to get up off the floor. "He had a gun and..." He stumbled to his jacket on a hook by the bathroom. "Drat! He got my wallet, my money."

"He robbed all of us," said Lola Grimm. "Did anyone get a good look?"

"Not me," said Frank, the manager. "He had on a cap, but... Maybe his hair was brown."

"I thought it was black," said Jim.

"I barely saw him," said Jonas, nursing the same kind of bruise that graced the heads of Jim and Frank. "He asked for my wallet. I pointed to my jacket. Then he hit me with his gun. I was out cold until one of you hit me with the door."

Sherman gave him a sheepish grin. "Sorry."

"We should call the police," said Frank. "The robber's probably miles away by now, but maybe we'll get lucky."

"Yes," Lola agreed. "Maybe he hasn't gone too far."

"He hasn't gone far at all," Sherman thought. "But I think I'll wait until the police arrive to make an accusation."

Who was the robber?
What clue revealed the robber's identity?

Solution on page 87.

Not For Sale

SHERMAN PARKED HIS ANTIQUE BENTLEY by the edge of the road, fascinated by the sight in front of him. True, the houses were not unusual, four comfortable residences built around a leafy cul-de-sac. The part Sherman found so fascinating was the signs on the lawns. The house on the right was graced with a real estate sign, "Contract Pending," printed in bold red. The house on the left boasted a similar sign [and a similar "Contract Pending"]. The house on the middle left had the same announcement springing from its grass.

The middle right house was different. The owner had

planted at least half a dozen placards in his front lawn. "Not For Sale," "Never For Sale," "Won't Sell. Don't Ask." "I'll Be Here Forever." All of them were hand-printed in an angry black scrawl.

"Someone doesn't want to move," Sherman chuckled to himself. "But unless I miss my guess, he or she has already been moved—from this world to the next."

Two police cars were parked behind each other in the double-wide driveway, while the other side was occupied by a van from the coroner's office. Sherman walked around to the backyard, just in time to see a pair of officers carrying a full black body bag toward the van's open doors.

"Sherman! Just the man I want to see." Sergeant Wilson, wearing plastic gloves, was in the yard. He had just picked up a bloody two-by-four and was placing it in an evidence bag. Below, on the grass, the rectangular piece of wood had left an outline of green in the middle of the blood-soaked lawn. "Murder weapon," he announced.

Wilson handed the blunt instrument to a patrolman, and then informed his friend of the facts. The deceased was Harry Ryder, owner of the "Not For Sale" house. Someone had attacked him in his yard, beating him to death.

"His neighbors were at home," Wilson added. "They're all suspects."

"Let me guess," Sherman said, rubbing his chin. "Someone wants to buy the entire cul-de-sac. But the deal will only go through if Mr. Ryder joins them and sells."

The sergeant nodded. "Some millionaire plans to tear down all four and build a mansion. Now that Ryder has been so conveniently killed, his heirs will sell and everyone will be happy. Except us, of course."

Sherman and Wilson went from home to home, interviewing the suspects. The owner of the far right house was Dan Osterling.

"I was out raking leaves," said the grizzled ex-Marine. "I saw Ryder come home around four. He parked in his garage and went directly inside. We didn't exchange a word. Two hours later, I'm in my den watching TV when the doorbell rings. It's you guys telling me that Ryder's been murdered."

The house on the far lef' was owned by Janet Vega, the real estate agent who'd put together the prospective sale. "I actually saw the attack," she told Wilson. "I was in my upstairs bedroom and didn't have my glasses on. But I saw a man clubbing Harry Ryder with a piece of wood. He kept hitting him until Harry stopped moving.

Then he wiped off the wood and threw it down beside the body. I called the police."

"And you couldn't tell who it was?" Wilson sounded doubtful.

"Sorry," Janet said. "He had on a baseball cap, so I couldn't even see his hair color."

The house on the middle left, right next to the victim's, was the property of Archie McDee, an out-of-work carpenter. "It's a shame Ryder was so stubborn," he told the homicide detective. "Janet put in so much effort to get us a great price, and then Ryder goes and spoils it all."

"Did you hear or see anything?" asked Wilson.

"Yeah," McDee admitted. "I had my side window open and I heard Ryder shouting for help. It sounded like he'd gotten himself into a fight. I probably should have called the cops, but I was mad. I figured he deserved whatever trouble he was in."

Wilson walked back to his car as mad as Sherman had ever seen him. "I never heard such bad alibis. I say they're all in this together, covering for each other."

"Well, one of them is definitely lying. Why don't we start there?"

Which suspect is lying?
How did Sherman know?

Solution on page 88.

Yes, Sir, That's My Bomb

SHERMAN SAT in Sergeant Wilson's homey but cluttered office reviewing a recent murder case, now closed. The sergeant was about to release a statement to the press and wanted to be sure he fully understood the brilliant deduction that he had supposedly made to solve it.

"Excuse me? Are you Sergeant Wilson?" A young, expensively dressed woman stood in the doorway. "I want to report a threat on my husband's life."

Her name was Amanda Sur, and her husband was John Sur, the real estate magnate who owned several blocks of Capital City's downtown district.

"Yesterday, we received this in the mail." Mrs. Sur handed the sergeant a note made up of cutout letters. "Prepare to Die, You Fat Old Parasite. Ka-Boom."

"Rather rude," sniffed Sherman.

Wilson looked over the note, then dismissed it as harmless. "A man like your husband must get threats all the time."

Mrs. Sur seemed taken aback. "No, this threat is serious. This morning I was at my kitchen window pouring coffee. The garage door was open and I saw someone inside there, skulking about. I sent John's nephew out to look, but by then, whoever it was must have left. My husband's life's in real danger."

"Have you thought about hiring a bodyguard?" asked Sherman.

"John refuses. He's not taking it seriously."

Sergeant Wilson was sympathetic but, as he told her, if her husband didn't take the threat seriously, there was little the police could do. He sent her away with a warning to keep her eyes open and call if she saw anything strange.

A few hours later, a call did come in, but it wasn't from Amanda. It was from an ambulance team parked outside the Sur residence. "There's been a car bomb explosion,"

the emergency worker informed them. "Both Mr. and Mrs. Sur were killed."

Holmes and Wilson arrived to find the mansion's garage a smoking, charred ruin. The victims inside the car had never stood a chance.

An EMS worker approached the sergeant. "We actually got a call from Mr. Sur, before the explosion. It seems his wife had tripped down the stairs and been knocked unconscious. He said he was going to drive her to the hospital. We told him to leave her alone, that we'd be there within ten minutes. But I guess he didn't want to wait."

Wilson nodded. "So, he puts his unconscious wife in the car, starts it up, and bam! It explodes. Whoever wanted to kill him got them both."

When the crime scene investigators finally showed up, Wilson and Sherman retreated into the mansion. They found the Sur nephew in the kitchen near the rear of the house. Kenny Sur had been at home all day. He verified the mailed threat and Amanda Sur's fears about an intruder.

"When was that car used last?" asked the sergeant.

"The one that exploded?" Kenny looked out the window and, although the wreckage wasn't visible, wisps smoke wafted from around the corner to remind them of the carnage. "That's their only car. The other one's in the shop. Amanda used it this morning to go to the police. It hasn't been used since."

"Were you here when she fell down the stairs?"

"Yeah," Kenny said. "She was knocked out cold. I told Uncle John to wait for the ambulance, but he refused. I helped him get her into the car. I was standing right outside the garage when it exploded." His face was still black with soot and there were cuts on his face and hands.

Wilson took his friend aside. "I feel terrible. The woman comes to us for protection and I send her home to get killed."

"I don't know exactly what happened," Sherman said. "But I've got a pretty good idea who was involved. You couldn't have prevented this."

What does Sherman suspect?
What evidence made him suspicious?

Solution on page 88.

The Voice Mail Alibi

THE CUTE LITTLE COUPE was parked off to the side of the country road just steps from a scenic waterfall. The contents of the car were neither cute nor scenic. A young woman sat in the driver's seat, her bloody head lolling out the open window. Sherman Holmes examined the bullet hole behind her ear.

"Want me to tell you how she died?" Sergeant Wilson could barely make himself heard above the roar of the falls. "The woman made a wrong turn and got lost. She stopped here. While she was parked, someone came up to the open window, shot her, then robbed her. Oh, and the time was exactly 2:17 p.m."

Sherman looked puzzled. Then his gaze fell on the open cell phone lying on the ground just outside the car window. "She was on the phone to someone; that's how you know the time?"

"Close," Wilson said. "She left a message on her brother's voice mail. He retrieved his messages around three and immediately called the police. Our boys started a search. They found her an hour later."

"I'd like to hear the voice mail message," Sherman said. "And meet the brother."

Sergeant Wilson drove his rotund, little friend across town to a cozy bungalow. Jerry Bass, the victim's brother, invited them inside. He was only a few years older than his sister, although grief made him appear older. Wilson asked if they could listen to the message and Jerry agreed.

A mechanized voice spoke first. "Message received today at—2:17 p.m."

"Connie here," a woman said. "Jerry, I'm going to be late." The connection was clear, with little interference or noise. "I'm taking a shortcut through Hopkins Forest and, of course, I got lost. I still have all my errands to do, so don't expect me... Hold on." Connie's voice changed. "What are you doing? No. No. Don't!" There was a deafening gunshot, followed by silence.

"Someone just came up to the car and shot her?" Sherman asked as he put down the receiver.

Jerry still appeared to be in shock. "If I didn't know better, I'd say it had to be Kurt, her ex-boyfriend."

"Yeah." Wilson frowned. "Tell my friend about Kurt."

Jerry turned to Sherman. "He's bad news. Connie broke up with him three times. They'd fight and he'd threaten her. But every time, she'd go back to him. I yelled at her so much. 'You gotta stay away from that loser.' She finally left him for good." Jerry sighed. "And now someone else kills her—for her rings and a few lousy bucks."

"What makes you think it isn't Kurt?" asked Sherman.

"I'll show you," Sergeant Wilson said and led the way out to the car.

They drove for fifteen minutes, stopping in front of a broken-down trailer surrounded by piles of debris. "This is Kurt's place. It's a good half-hour from that spot in Hopkins Forest. This afternoon, the Brothers of Mercy were canvassing the area for donations. Brother Dominic swears—as much as a religious man can swear—that he was speaking to Kurt right here at 2:30 today. He remembers because Kurt pushed him off the trailer porch and broke his watch."

"And his watch was set to the correct time?"

"Yes."

Sherman thought for a moment, then smiled. "You don't have to worry about alibis. I'm sure your crime scene people will come to the same conclusion I just did."

What does Sherman suspect?
What lead him to that conclusion?

Solution on page 89.

The Moriarty Note

"YOU'RE NOT REALLY A BELIEVER, are you?"
Agatha stared deeply into Sherman's eyes.

"Not really," the little detective admitted somewhat sheepishly. "But I do enjoy our evenings together."

"That's the most important thing," Luther said as he started clearing the dinner table.

"We enjoy your company, too," added Grimelda, helping Luther with the plates. "Although it would be nice if you trusted the spirit world."

Once a week, for the last few years, Sherman and his friends had gathered at one of their houses for an evening of food, drink and spiritualism. Luther, Agatha, and Grimelda were amateur witches who took their magic seriously. Sherman came for the companionship and fun. Tonight they were at Luther's home, where the after-dinner entertainment was to be a séance.

One by one, the host and his guests trickled into the pantry that Luther had turned into a spirit room. Agatha was the last one in. She closed the door behind her and joined the others around the small, round table. They all clasped hands, and the others watched as Agatha went into an impressive trance. Their goal tonight was to contact Professor Moriarty, the archenemy of Sherman's great-great-grandfather. On two previous occasions, they had tried to contact Sherlock Holmes himself and once they'd tried John Watson, the great detective's assistant.

Agatha chanted and moaned and called on her spirit contacts for help. For long minutes, nothing happened, and then came a sharp rap, like a knock on the door. The witches grew excited and Agatha doubled her efforts to summon the arch-villain. But there was nothing more. This attempt, like their previous ones, ended in failure. The self-proclaimed witch came out of her trance and weakly asked for a glass of water. Grimelda opened the door and went out to the kitchen while the others sat quietly.

"It's because you're a doubter," Grimelda said to Sherman on her return. There was a touch of blame in her voice. Agatha sipped her water, then everyone rose from the table.

Sherman was halfway through the living room when he heard a gasp. He turned around to see Luther by the pantry/spirit room. Luther had just closed the door and Sherman could see him pulling something out of the

wood surface. It was a note and a knife that had held it in place. "From the spirits," he whispered.

"That rap we heard," said Grimelda, with growing excitement. "What does it say?" She grabbed the note and read. "Seek not to disturb my soul. I will not warn you again. Moriarty."

"You see?" Agatha said. "This proves it. The spirits are real."

Sherman shook his head. "The only thing it proves is that one of you is playing a joke on me."

"No," Grimelda insisted. "There was no note on the door when we went in."

That was true. Sherman had opened the door himself and there hadn't been anything stuck in it. "One of you put it there later," Sherman said. "Let me see."

The knife was short and sharp, probably from the kitchen. The message was written in black ink and the paper was creased as if it had been folded. A tear in the center showed where it had been held in place. The door, Sherman saw, was made of hardwood, thick and tough. The wound made by the knife was barely visible, but it was there, deeper than Sherman would have thought.

"I don't appreciate the joke," Sherman said, focusing on one of his friends in particular. "It's one thing to believe in spirits. It's another to try to trick someone into sharing your belief."

Who planted the note and the knife?
How did Sherman know which friend it was?

Solution on page 90

Home Office Homicide

"VERY NEATLY DRESSED," Sherman observed as the medical examiner gently turned the body face up and began a preliminary examination.

The victim was wearing a dark, custom-made suit with a fresh rosebud in his lapel. The only thing marring the outfit was the gash left by the silver letter opener that had been placed in his back. That and the blood.

Sergeant Wilson led his friend to the far side of the elegant office. The dead lawyer, Patrick Wales, Esquire, ran his firm out of the first floor of his home, a beautifully restored structure in the heart of Capital City's best neighborhood.

"At least we know the time of death," Wilson said, pointing to the phone lying beside the body. "At 8:55 this

morning, Wales telephoned his accountant. At 9:05, the accountant heard Wales scream and that was it—end of conversation. The accountant called for help and they called us."

"A single thrust in the back," observed Sherman. "Who else was in the house?"

"Three individuals," Wilson said, checking his notes. "The deceased's wife, his law partner, and their assistant."

Holmes and Wilson wandered out of the office and into the front hall. A woman in her mid-forties dressed in a white bathrobe stood anxiously by a flower arrangement on the center table.

"I'm Lydia Wales," she said in a flat, even voice. "My husband and I were upstairs in our suite. Patrick finished dressing around 8:30, and then went downstairs. I was still in my bathroom when I heard him scream."

Lydia was about to continue when a tall, sandy-haired man entered from the direction of the kitchen. He introduced himself as Jake Martin, law partner of the decedent. "I walked through the front door around 8:30," Martin said when asked his whereabouts at the time. "Just as Patrick was coming downstairs. The two of us went into the kitchen for some coffee. Shortly before nine, Patrick left to make a phone call—in private. I went out back to have a cigarette. I was out there when I heard his scream."

The legal assistant was the last to be interviewed. "I got here right at 9:00," said Penny DeLoren, an attractive young woman in a seriously ambitious suit. "I bring in flowers every Monday," she said, pointing to the roses on the hall table. "The office door was closed. I was in the library when I heard Patrick scream."

Sergeant Wilson pointed to the "No Smoking" sign on the hall table, then led Sherman out to the front porch. Neither man smoked, but they needed to talk.

Wilson spoke first. "The guy Wales called, the accountant, says the victim was paranoid about money. Wales was whining about embezzlement and demanded a full financial review. The accountant didn't take him seriously, but..."

"But Wales may have been right," Sherman said as he puffed on his unlit pipe. "Are you ready to make an arrest?"

Who killed Patrick Wales?
What clue gave the killer away?

Solution on page 91.

Sherman on the Scene

"**Y**OU'RE THE CRIME SCENE TECHNICIAN?" Sherman asked the slovenly, middle-aged man who had just arrived at the front door of the murder site. "May I see some I.D?"

The man was dressed in a police windbreaker and carried a crime kit. He flipped open his wallet and showed the laminated identification. It was a well-worn card, and the photo was curling slightly at its edge. The photo matched the man's face and Sherman let him in.

Despite all the crime scenes the pudgy detective had visited, he'd rarely been left alone at one. But five minutes ago, Wilson and his men had been called away to deal with a confirmed sighting of the perp. Sherman wasn't all that fond of car chases and opted to remain at the scene.

"A technician's coming," Wilson informed him as he and his men left. "Don't let anyone else in."

"Which room?" The technician looked bored but competent.

Sherman led him towards the back of the impressive house, talking as he went. "The victim is Oliver Lasky, a corporate bigwig. The killer broke in and bypassed the security system. That, combined with other facts, makes me think it was a hired professional."

They walked into the sumptuously decorated bedroom. A man in his early forties lay just inside the bathroom, a ribbon of red trailing from a single gunshot wound to the head. The bedroom itself was a mess—broken lamps, torn sheets, feathers from a burst pillow.

The technician played with the corners of his mustache. "What a mess."

Sherman shrugged. "Mr. Lasky saw him coming and put up a struggle. The maid and the gardener arrived in the middle of all this. They heard the gunshot and saw the killer running out the back. They gave us a rough description. In his rush, the killer might have left something—fingerprint, hair follicle, bullet casing..."

"Well, that's my job," said the technician. He was putting on gloves and opening his crime kit when the doorbell rang again.

Sherman left him to his work and returned to the front door. A woman wrapped in a fur stood on the front porch,

leaning against a marble column. Leaning against another column was a youngish man in a hand-tailored suit.

"The police informed me of my husband's death," the woman said coolly as she tried to push her way inside. "I want to see him."

"Mrs. Lasky," Sherman said. It wasn't much of a deduction. "I believe you and your husband were estranged." That wasn't much of a deduction either.

"He's still my husband and this is still my house. Let me in."

The youngish man now stepped forward. "I'm Mr. Lasky's business partner, Ed Burton," he said with an ingratiating smile. "Are you with the police?"

"I'm with them, yes," Sherman answered. "And I can't let anyone in."

"This is illegal," Mrs. Lasky fumed.

"Actually, it's not," said Sherman. He continued to hold his ground, preventing the widow and the partner from gaining entry. This standoff ended when Sherman's cell phone rang. He closed the door in their faces before answering.

"Sherman?" It was Sergeant Wilson. "We've found another victim. It's an unidentified man killed behind a strip mall about a mile from you. A witness described the same sort of man seen by the maid."

Sherman thought for a moment. "Sergeant, come back here. Now. There's someone you need to talk to."

What does Sherman suspect?
What triggered his suspicion?

Solution on page 91.

Blackmail Can be Deadly

SHERMAN WAS ANGRY and fully prepared to yell at someone. This morning he'd heard that the post office was issuing a new stamp, celebrating the career of his great-great grandfather. That would have been wonderful news, quite wonderful indeed, except that the new Sherlock Holmes stamp was to be part of a series commemorating fictional heroes. And, as Sherman told anyone who would listen, his ancestor was in no way fictional.

Sherman strutted into the main post office building, only to see three other people at the counter, yelling at the city's postmaster. The diminutive detective recognized one of them. It was Harry Beam, his next door neighbor.

Harry waved him to join them. "This is Sherman Holmes," he announced to the others. "From over on Maple Street. Sherman, we need to find out who rents P.O. Box 447."

"I cannot divulge that information," the postmaster said with a shrug.

"Why do you need to know?" Sherman asked his neighbor.

"Can we trust him?" whispered the woman in the group.

"Absolutely," said Harry. "He's a private detective."

The three took Sherman aside to privately explain their predicament. "I received an anonymous letter this morning," said the woman. She had introduced herself as Joyce. "It was blackmail. The snake knew things about me. Bad things. The letter told me to send five hundred dollars a month to Post Office Box 447. I came right over here to find out who it is."

"I had the same experience," said Harry with obvious embarrassment. "I don't know how the blackmailer found out. When I got here, I found Joyce already trying to get information about the box."

"I got here a minute or so later," said the other man. "My name's Bill. And don't tell us to go to the police. I'd rather pay than have the police find out about me."

"How do you think the blackmailer discovered your secrets?" asked Sherman.

"I don't know," said Joyce. "We're all strangers to each other. We might have been involved in the same sort of activity—the thing we're being blackmailed for—but that's just a guess."

Sherman was intrigued by the situation, but didn't hold out much hope. "Even if you discover the blackmailer's identity, it won't do you any good, not unless you go to the police."

"Maybe we can do something," said Harry darkly. "Maybe we can take matters into our own hands."

Bill nodded. "If you have any ideas on how to catch him, Mr. Holmes, just tell your neighbor here. We'll give him our phone numbers."

Sherman wasn't too worried. He honestly didn't think they would do anything illegal. But that same evening, he heard about the murder on the news.

His next-door neighbor, Harry O'Doul, had been found shot dead in a downtown alley. According to the local newscaster, there had been a struggle, and Harry had been shot at close range with his own gun.

Sherman flipped off the TV and sat in the dark, thinking. Had Harry really done what he'd threatened? Had he discovered the blackmailer's identity and gone after that person with a gun? Sherman thought for a few more minutes, then reached for his phone and pressed #1 on his speed dial.

"Sergeant Wilson? I hear you have another murder. I'd like to help out if I may."

What does Sherman suspect?
What aroused his suspicions?

Solution on page 92.

Message from the Grave

A TOWEL HAD BEEN WEDGED underneath the door, so it took more than a little effort to push it open.

"Hold your breath," Sergeant Wilson said to the men behind him as he pushed his way into the bedroom.

Directly behind him was a team of paramedics. They rushed to the man lying by the gas fireplace, while Wilson turned off the gas valve, then ran for the windows, unlocking them one by one and throwing them open. Throughout all this, Sherman Holmes remained in the hallway, holding his breath.

The two paramedics worked for several minutes before giving up. "He's dead," Wilson confirmed with a sigh. "You can come in now, Sherman—and breathe."

Sherman entered the small, elegant bedroom, taking in the full scene. A baseball bat lay not far from the body, a towel still partly wrapped around it, doing away with the possibility of prints. The only other door opened into a private bathroom. Wilson had just unlocked and opened the window in that room, turning on the exhaust fan for good measure.

Sherman looked at the bruise on Ben Hunter's left temple, at the blue, asphyxiated lips, and finally at the open cell phone in his hand. "If he'd called the police instead of his son's home, he might still be alive."

"Maybe, maybe not," said Wilson. "My guess is the killer slugged him with the baseball bat, then turned on the gas and left. The victim recovered just enough strength to grab the phone from his pocket and press the first number on his speed dial. He wouldn't have to give his son the address or other information, unlike the police. A smart move, except that his son wasn't home."

"I'm never home on weekdays," came a voice from behind them in the doorway. In all the turmoil, they'd forgotten about the deceased's two relatives. Doug Hunter, the son in question, was staring at his father's lifeless body. "I guess he was too confused to remember. I did call my home voice mail and got the message, but it was too late."

"Ben's had some health problems," said the other relative. "And he's been depressed. Are you sure he didn't commit suicide?"

It was Ben Hunter's wife—estranged wife, as she insisted on pointing out. Carla Hunter was a full decade younger than the corpse with the blue lips.

"It doesn't look that way," said Sergeant Wilson. "As his wife, you inherit his estate. Is that correct?"

"What's left of it," said Carla. "Ben's business went bankrupt last year. If you're looking for someone with a motive, try Doug. Ben changed his insurance to make his son the beneficiary. I believe the policy pays double if Ben was murdered or died by violence."

"That's true," Doug admitted. "But I was at work all morning. You can check with my supervisor at the plant."

Sherman nodded. The lingering smell of gas made him more nervous than he otherwise would have been.

"Can you access the voice mail message your father left? I'd like to hear it."

Doug Hunter said "Sure," then flipped open his own cell phone and punched in a long series of numbers. He handed the phone to Sherman.

"Someone hit me." The voice was weak, the connection bad. "Bedroom. Gas. Don't know who. Still in the house. In the hall. Hurry." Sherman listened to the message twice, then handed the phone back to Doug.

"Well?" Sergeant Wilson took his friend aside, toward one of the open windows. "You think one of them hired someone? A hit man?"

Sherman shook his head. "There's more to this case than meets the eye."

Who was responsible for Ben Hunter's death?
What clue alerted Sherman?

Solution on page 93.

Death of a Diva

WITH HIS PLASTIC GLOVES ON, Sergeant Wilson lifted the victim's head from the make-up table and gently turned it. "Was she from India?" he asked, a note of confusion in his voice. Pressed into the middle of the woman's forehead was a glittering red dot.

Sherman Holmes examined the dot. "No." He almost chuckled. "That's a sequin." And he pointed to the red-sequined costume on a hanger in the corner.

The police detective and his amateur assistant were in a private dressing room, backstage at the newly built Melody Dinner Theater on Highway 11. The victim was Leona Hempsted, a bleached blonde matron carrying a few too many pounds and wrinkles. According to Tommy Burton, the theater owner, Leona had been cast as the star of his first show, Broadway Spangles. She was also his biggest investor. The detectives exited the dressing room, only to face a herd of actors and technicians gathered in the hall.

"Who discovered the body?" Wilson asked.

The theater owner stepped forward. "Tonight was our first dress rehearsal," Tommy said. "I arrived late with the costumes, around 7 p.m. I went right to the dressing rooms in the basement and handed them out. The actors tried them on. They loved them. Then I came up here with Jake, my nephew." He pointed out a fifteen-year-old boy dressed in a blue-sequined jumpsuit. "Leona has the only dressing room on the stage level. We knocked. When there was no answer, we came in and found her body. We didn't touch a thing."

Wilson nodded then said, "Looks like there was a fight," which was something of an understatement. The dressing room was in shambles, with a broken mirror, scattered flowers and shattered vases. The red from a gash on Leona's head matched the red on the seat of a stool that lay cracked on the bloody carpet.

"Leona had a temper," Tommy admitted. "She never let us forget whose money paid the bills."

"Excuse me? Tommy?" A young woman in a red-sequined costume raised her hand. "Does this mean I get the lead, now that she's dead?" Her name, they soon learned, was Diane Walsh, and she didn't even pretend to

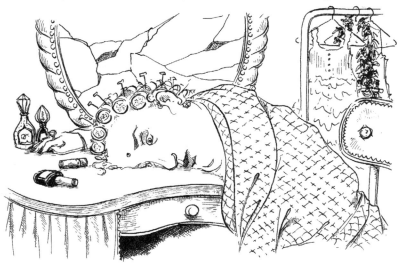

be upset by the murder. "Leona was a terrible singer and a worse human being. She fought with everyone."

"Did you fight with her?" asked Sherman.

"Not today. I got here around 6:30. Leona was in the lot, parked in a handicap space. She was unloading flowers—from admirers, she said, although I'm sure she sent them herself. I helped carry them to her dressing room. Then I went downstairs. I was there with the other girls in our crowded little dressing room until Tommy and his nephew came back down with the news."

"Did anyone hear the fight?" asked Sergeant Wilson.

A tall, nervous-looking man stepped forward. "I'm Ollie Reese, the director. I got here at 6:30, too. I saw Leona and Diane in the parking lot with the flowers. I went directly backstage and started working on light cues. I did hear Leona screaming at someone and glass breaking. But that wasn't unusual. To be honest, I didn't want to get in the middle of another fight, so I ignored it."

"When did you hear this fight?" asked Sherman.

"Just a few minutes before seven."

Everyone else, it turned out, had been in the basement or too far away, so there was no one to support Ollie Reese's estimate of the murder time.

Wilson took his friend aside. "It could have been anyone in the building. We've got a long night ahead of us, Sherm."

"Not necessarily," Sherman said. "We've only talked to three people and I already know one of them is lying."

Which suspect is lying?
How did Sherman know?

Solution on page 94.

Solutions

The British Maid

Sergeant Wilson stopped in his tracks. "How do you get here before me?" he growled. "If I didn't know better, I'd say you were Capital City's biggest criminal."

The sergeant turned to his men and barked a series of commands. The officers put on gloves and fanned out over the scene. "You've taken me to this restaurant, Holmes. Is that the owner?"

"Owner and chef. Unfortunately, the establishment might not be able to survive without Henry Bull and his prep chef."

"Prep...? Don't tell me there were two murders?"

"No, just one. The prep chef, Hugo, is the killer."

"How do you know that?"

"Look at the knife in the victim." Sherman paused while the sergeant did as he was told. "Does it have a long blade or a short one? Is it a paring knife or something else, like a steak knife?"

"How should I know? The blade's in the victim."

"Exactly. And yet Hugo knew which knife it was—a short paring knife."

Wilson thought it over and then shook his head. "Maybe Hugo saw which knife was missing."

"No. All three suspects said they'd just arrived. And all the knives have exactly the same handles. Like it or not, Hugo's your man."

A Country Crime

"I'm afraid I can't take full credit for this one," Sherman said with a modest smile.

"Course not," Wilson snapped. "We're partners—well, not in an official sense."

"Exactly. And thanks for giving me the solution."

"What solution?" Wilson demanded. "How did I give it to you?"

"You're the one who pointed out the burrs on our trousers."

"Well, yes, they're pretty obvious. And annoying."

"Anyone walking across that field would get his clothing covered with them, don't you think?" He didn't wait for an answer. "And yet Glenda's black skirt looks perfectly neat and clean."

Sergeant Wilson turned to eye the clothing in question. "You're right. She couldn't have walked across the field to get here."

"And her clothing is dry, so she didn't ford the river. I suspect Glenda was the passenger Billy Bob saw in the victim's pickup. That places her out here with him around the time he was killed."

"I'm glad you picked up on my clue." Wilson beamed. "Sometimes it takes a city boy to solve a country crime."

The Halloween Devil

"I don't know how you do it," Wilson said with obvious relief. "Both alibis are weak. Either one of these guys could have been in that costume."

"Oh, it wasn't them," Sherman chuckled. "It was the suspect you didn't meet, the guy in the vacant lot."

"The other victim?" Wilson asked, his bushy eyebrows raised. "But he's got serious stab wounds. Are you saying he did that to himself?"

"Oh, no. Someone stabbed him. The girl. You said she fought back, correct?"

"You're saying he stripped off the costume and ran into the lot, pretending to be a victim?" Wilson wasn't buying it. "No. Why didn't he just run away? Why draw so much attention to himself?"

"Because he needed medical help. If a man showed up at the hospital tonight with an unexplained stab wound…"

"He'd be a suspect, of course. Do you have any evidence to back up this wild theory?"

"I do. This supposed victim said he'd been chased into the lot, then attacked. Yet I found only one set of footprints going in and no footprints coming out."

"Maybe you missed seeing them."

"If someone is chasing you, his footprints are going to be fairly close to yours. No, your forensics team will back me up. That so-called victim is your killer."

Murder on Vacation

The bellhop had to ask. "Who was your great-great grandfather?"

"Just the world's greatest detective," Sherman answered modestly. "But even I know enough to ask a few questions, like why tie a rock around the gun? Did the killer really need a rock to make it sink? And why use a handkerchief? True, the gun would produce gunshot residue, but washing your hands would have easily eliminated that evidence.

"And most important." He walked out onto the balcony. "What caused this nick in the stone railing? The answer, of course, is the gun. Mary McDill draped the rope and the weight over the balcony. After she shot herself, the weight pulled the gun over the railing and into the sea, damaging the stone edge as it went."

"You're saying Ms. McDill killed herself?"

"She did. She meant to lure Sonny to her room at six o'clock.

As soon as she heard the knock on her door, she screamed out his name and shot herself. She'd planned for him to get caught on the scene. But he'd gotten caught in traffic instead. As for the handkerchief, she used it to protect her hand from the tell-tale residue."

"And the handkerchief just floated down to the other balcony?"

"Yes. I recommend 'The Problem of Thor Bridge' for your reading enjoyment. That's the case my great-great grandfather solved."

The Hostess Stumbles

"They say she'll live," Delia sighed, as they paced the emergency room, feeling useless.

"For now," Sherman said. "Until someone makes another try."

Lucas frowned. "Are you saying someone tried to kill Alice?"

"Oh, yes. The bridge was booby-trapped, just waiting for her to cross it."

Bernie shook his head. "It could have been any one of us crossing that bridge. What makes you think she was the target?"

Delia stopped her pacing. "You know, Sherman. Before she left, Alice looked at you rather accusingly."

"That confused me, too," said Sherman, "but I figured it out. It's first thing in the morning. Our hostess goes into the kitchen, says 'drat', then grabs her car keys and says she'll be back in a minute. What does that say to you?"

Delia pondered. "If it were me, I would be out of milk, or coffee, or something."

"Exactly. And you'd probably throw a wicked glance at the guest you thought just drank a full gallon of milk."

"You drank a gallon of milk?"

"No. Someone was in the kitchen after me. He poured the milk down the sink, figuring that Alice would do just what she did, race out to buy another gallon."

"What do you mean, 'he'?" Bernie asked.

"I mean you," Sherman said. "Delia and Lucas came down from upstairs. But you showed up with a cup of coffee, meaning you were probably in the kitchen after me. Only you could have thrown the milk away."

Found Money

Sherman bit into his sandwich and chewed thoroughly before speaking. "If you're going to bring someone in for questioning, I'd choose the guy in the sweaty tracksuit. But you'd better be careful. He's a boxer."

The boxer had finished lunch and was wiping his mouth. "All right," Wilson whispered. "Tell me quickly."

"Because today is Wednesday and he's running."

Wilson sighed. "All right, tell me slowly."

"Our dimwitted athlete went to great lengths to explain his training schedule." If anything, Sherman spoke even slower than normal. "A day in the gym, then a day sparring, then a day of road work. No days off. If you work backwards from today, that makes last Thursday a running day. He could have found the bag and picked it up."

"Could have?" Wilson snorted. "Could have?"

"I know," Sherman agreed. "Hardly conclusive. Except he lied. He told me he went jogging last Wednesday, not Thursday."

"Maybe he got mixed up."

"He remembered that Wednesday was his jogging day and his birthday. Either he's confused about his birthday…"

"All right," Wilson said and pushed himself to his feet. "But if he punches me, I'm punching you."

Crime in Record Time

The sergeant seemed confused. "What do you mean, record time? You've solved plenty of crimes faster than this."

"It's a pun, Wilson. I was referring to time itself—or, more accurately, a clock." Sherman pointed to the digital clock on the end table. "During the storm last night, the power went off. When it came back on, what do you suppose happened to this clock?"

Wilson shrugged. "It's a digital clock. I suppose it reset itself at twelve midnight. That's what my clocks do."

"Right. And yet this clock is only a few minutes off. I didn't reset it to the correct time."

"What about Howard?"

"After we found the body, he collapsed in the gazebo. I don't think he went around the house resetting clocks. The logical explanation is that the power went back on just around midnight."

"That's not what you told the cops."

"I told them what Joey told me, that it was 11:30 when the power went on and he drove off. But that was a lie. It was really around midnight, which gave Joey enough time to kill Eliza after the 11:45 train passed by."

Wilson Wins One

"Congratulations," Sherman said with as much grace as he could muster. "Of course you had a piece of information I didn't."

"True," Wilson admitted. "It's quite elementary." He was nearly champing at the bit. "Do you want me to explain it?"

"No need," Sherman said, with a good imitation of a yawn. "Now that you've confirmed that you had information I didn't, the answer is child's play. The thief was Melanie."

Wilson was crestfallen. "How did you know?"

"Elementary, as you said. The one thing you did here that I didn't was shake hands with Melanie. I imagine her hand was sticky."

"Yeah," Wilson growled. "It was."

"Sticky from putting the bag in the crevice. The shop's bathroom isn't working, so she couldn't have washed it off. Since you admitted having information I didn't, that was the only possibility."

"I solved this one on my own, Holmes. Don't try to take credit for it."

"I never do."

"I know." Wilson pouted. His success left him frustrated. How could he brag about finally besting Sherman Holmes when Wilson always took credit anyway?

Murder Works Weekends

"Was it Loose?" Wilson asked eagerly. "The guy with the golf club in his office?"

"No," Sherman said. "Just because a suspect goofs off doesn't mean he's a killer. I think our solution lies in those background documents Miss Draw put together."

Wilson's eyes gleamed. "You mean it had something to do with this lawsuit?"

"No. Look at the number of copies. How many were in the pile that Loose picked up from the document center?"

"One for each person. Three."

"So, why did Penelope Draw make three copies when there were going to be four people in the meeting—the three of them plus the deceased?"

Wilson thought for a second, then grinned. "The lady was in a rush. She had to get her copies made, then go in and kill her senior partner. She didn't have time to put together a fourth document that would never get used. It's elementary, Holmes, elementary."

Door-to-Door Homicide

"I hate it when you smile like that," Wilson snarled. "Okay, who was it?"

"It was the niece, Nan Waterford."

"What?" Wilson scrunched up his face. "And the motive?"

"I don't know," Sherman admitted. "She was the victim's closest relation. Perhaps she inherited. The old lady was going to visit her lawyer. Perhaps she intended to change her will. Have your men check it out."

"Okay. Forget motive. How did she do it?"

"Nan dropped by earlier, sometime after both door-to-door men had left. Perhaps 1:45. That's when she killed her aunt. She made it look like a robbery, then drove off and returned a few minutes later, making sure she had a neighbor around this time to witness her discovery of the body."

"That's pure conjecture," Wilson said under his breath.

"Not really," Sherman said, as irritatingly cool as ever. "There were no prints on the answering machine."

"So? The killer wiped the machine."

"Why?"

"Because?" Wilson had to think. "Because the killer's prints were on the machine."

"Why?"

"Because the killer erased a message?" Wilson guessed.

"Exactly. None of the other suspects knew the victim's phone number. If your electronics wizards can do some magic on that machine, they'll find an earlier message from Nan, very similar to the one that's on there now."

"But with an earlier time stamp. Maybe 1:45."

"Exactly."

What the Killer Forgot

Sherman Holmes crooked a finger at Longo. The tall, young officer crossed to his side and bent down, his ear within an inch of Sherman's mouth. "Do as I say," Sherman whispered. Longo nodded. "Arrest Officer Maloney."

Longo stood up slowly. A second later, his side arm was drawn and aimed at the beefy giant. "Maloney, you're under arrest."

"What?" Maloney blustered. "You're kidding."

"Afraid not," said Sherman. "You arrived early for your shift, for a meeting with Wheeler. You killed him. My guess is you got blood on you and took a quick shower. We'll check the clothes in your locker."

"That's ridiculous," said Maloney.

"You left by the emergency exit, but you made one mistake."

"Guys, you can't believe this little freak."

"You forgot your watch."

"What are you talking about? I got my watch right here."

"I know. But when I met you in the vestibule, you didn't have it. You asked me for the time. While the other two went out to get me, you retrieved your watch and put it on."

"No," Maloney protested. "I left my watch here at the end of yesterday's shift."

"But you've been on vacation for a week." Officer Longo smiled. "Good work, Shermie."

"Thanks," Sherman said with a little bow. "Now stop calling me Shermie."

Crime at Criminy Woods

The deputy sheriff who arrived had been skeptical about Sherman Holmes's credentials, but a call to Capital City was very persuasive. "Sergeant Wilson says I'm to arrest the person you point out. He's got a lot of faith in you."

"That's very nice of him," Sherman said with as much modesty as he could muster. "Don't worry. I'm right. In fact, if you'll look in the trunk of Jonas Boatman's car, I imagine you'll find everything he stole."

"How do you know that?"

"It's logical. No one would think of searching the cars of the victims."

"But Boatman was hit, like the other two."

"Self-inflicted, my dear man. There is no way his story happened the way he said."

"But his story's the same as the others'. A demand for money, a hit on the head."

"Yes," Sherman said. "But he also said he was knocked cold until I hit him with the door. That couldn't be. I mean, if his body was blocking the door, how did the robber get out?"

Sherman and the deputy were in one of the cabins, an exact duplicate of the others. "The windows are small," Sherman said. "The only way to explain how the robber got out without pushing Boatman out of the way is simple. There was no robber."

Not for Sale

"I say they're all lying," Sergeant Wilson insisted.

"Maybe," said Sherman. "But we know for sure that Janet Vega didn't see Ryder being hit with that two-by-four."

"How do we know that?"

"Well, for one thing, the two-by-four wasn't the murder weapon."

Wilson stopped in his tracks, his mouth falling open. "What? It was a bloody, blunt instrument, lying right by the body."

Sherman nodded in agreement. "But it wasn't the weapon. That piece of wood was on the ground when the attack happened. That's the only way it could have left an outline of green when you picked it up. The forensics team will confirm this. Meanwhile, you should bring in Ms. Vega for questioning. Either she killed Ryder herself or saw a completely different scene from the one she told us about."

Yes, Sir, That's My Bomb

"I should have listened to her," Wilson berated himself. "But the threat sounded so unconvincing."

"It was unconvincing," Sherman agreed, "because she made it up. My guess is Mrs. Sur was planning to kill her husband. She constructed a note and a story about seeing someone sneaking around the garage. When her husband died in an explosion, we were supposed to believe it was some enemy."

Wilson shook his head. "But Amanda Sur also died."

"So? She was unconscious, unable to prevent her husband from putting her in the car. Unless I miss my guess, Mrs. Sur died from her own bomb."

For once, Wilson was speechless.

"She may have had an accomplice," Sherman continued. "You should check into that."

"And what makes you think Mrs. Sur made up the story about the intruder?"

"Elementary. She said she saw into the garage from her kitchen window. But that's impossible. The garage is all the way around the corner from the kitchen window."

Sherman proved to be right, of course. Kenny and Amanda were in it together, planning to split John Sur's money on his death. When Amanda was knocked out, Kenny figured it was his lucky break. He would no longer have to share.

The Voice Mail Alibi

"And what conclusion did you come to?" Sergeant Wilson asked.

"That the body was moved," Sherman replied. "Connie Bass did not die where she was found."

"What are you talking about?" Wilson didn't try to hide his amusement. "We have Connie's voice, saying she was lost in the forest, followed by the gunshot."

"Connie was lying, telling her brother she was someplace she wasn't."

"Why would she do that?"

"Because she was with Kurt; that's my guess. Why else would she lie about a simple thing like her location? Her brother yelled at her whenever she went back to Kurt, remember?"

"And what makes you think the body was moved?"

"Because there's no waterfall sound on the tape. You and I could barely hear each other over the roar. Connie supposedly had the window rolled down and yet there's no background noise.

"My guess is they were fighting before she called her brother. Kurt heard her lying and that must have triggered his anger. Afterwards, after Brother Dominic dropped by, Kurt realized he had an alibi. All he had to do was transport the body to where Connie said she'd been."

The Moriarty Note

"Why are you looking at me?" Luther asked. "I couldn't have put the note on the door. Grimelda was the only one to leave the room. If a human did it, it was her."

"I didn't," protested Grimelda. "If anyone did it, it was Agatha. She was the last to enter. She could have done it then."

"It couldn't have been either of you." Sherman was emphatic. "Even if you had the time and the luck to do it without being seen, the act of stabbing the door would have made a sound. We all would have heard it."

"We all did hear it," Agatha said. "That sound when we were at the table. That was Moriarty's spirit stabbing the door."

Sherman smirked. "That was Luther, rapping the bottom of the table."

"Wait a minute." Agatha scratched her head. "Luther must be eliminated, too. No one could have stabbed it without making a sound. It was Moriarty."

"It was Luther," Sherman said. "And the reason he didn't make a sound was he never stabbed the door. Luther was the last to leave the séance room. He took the note from one pocket, the knife from another, then pretended he was just taking them down. As for the stab mark, he had made that earlier. This is his house, remember?"

Grimelda looked at Luther, who stared back defiantly, refusing to admit anything. "I guess that's possible," she said. "But I still think it was the spirit of Moriarty."

Home Office Homicide

"I don't suppose you buy roses very often," Sherman said. He was pointing through the front window to the roses on the hall table.

"Sure," Wilson said. "Once a year on our anniversary—when I remember."

"And how long do roses stay fresh?"

"Three or four days." Wilson had to remind himself that Sherman's aimless digressions usually led somewhere.

"So an unopened rosebud would probably be less than a week old."

"Look, Shermy, what's your point?"

"My point is Penny DeLoren brought in roses this morning, and the victim was found with a rosebud in his lapel."

"So? He picked a rose from the bouquet."

"And how did that happen? Wales got on the phone at 8:55 a.m. and never got off. Penny says she arrived with the flowers at 9:00. When did Wales have time to pick a flower and put it in his lapel?"

Wilson thought it over. "Penny arrived earlier, when the victim and his partner were in the kitchen having coffee. Wales then picked the bud, went into his office and got on the phone. Penny must have been walking by and heard him talking about embezzlement."

Sherman smiled. "Let's go in and have a talk with Ms. DeLoren."

Sherman on the Scene

Nervously, Sherman waited in the front room. Every instinct but duty told him to flee the scene. Less than a minute later, Wilson and his men drove up. Sherman ran out to greet them, nearly knocking over Mrs. Lasky on the way. "I'm sorry, I'm sorry," he shouted. "I let the killer into the crime scene."

"You did what?" Wilson shouted back.

"He must have left some evidence in the bedroom. He came back to destroy it."

Wilson motioned his men to go around back, then drew his gun and entered the house. "What are you talking about?"

"That body you found at the strip mall. I'm guessing that's the real crime scene technician. The assassin killed him, then took his equipment. He went to a photo machine in the strip mall and changed the man's I.D. Then he came here, pretending to be the technician. I let him in."

Sherman's explanation was interrupted by the sound of gunfire from behind the house. Both men waited. "Sarge?" a voice called out. "We got him."

"Thank goodness," Sherman sighed. "I should have known his I.D. was fake. The card was laminated, and yet the photo was curling at the edge. Obviously, he glued his own, new photo on top of the real technician's photo."

Blackmail Can Be Deadly

Sherman arrived at the precinct house in a state of agitation and marched straight into the sergeant's office.

"I blame myself," Sherman said before Wilson could even say hello. "Harry O'Doul was my neighbor. I should have been able to piece it together."

"Don't blame yourself," Wilson said. "You couldn't have known O'Doul was being blackmailed."

"I did know," Sherman said.

"Oh." Wilson looked confused. "Do you know why? We found Harry O'Doul's diary. Turns out he torched his company's building last year to collect on the insurance. No one knew except for the person blackmailing him."

"I didn't know about the arson," Sherman admitted. "But the blackmailer calls himself Bill. Harry knew this and went to attack him. I imagine Bill acted in self-defense."

"Interesting," said Wilson. "What do you know about this Bill?"

"I can describe him," Sherman said. "I assume he used to work for the arson squad. That's how he knew about the fire. He was also blackmailing a woman named Joyce. When Bill went to check on his post office box, he found Harry and Joyce already there, so he pretended to be another victim of the blackmailer."

"And how did Harry know about Bill?"

"That's the part I should have known. When Harry introduced us, he told Bill I live on Maple Street. Bill supposedly knew nothing about Harry. They were strangers. And yet Bill called us neighbors. He somehow knew that Harry lived on Maple, too."

Message from the Grave

Sergeant Wilson had a fairly easy job. The hardest parts were putting up with his eccentric friend, and then convincing the D.A. to prosecute the right person. "Who should I bring in for questioning?" he asked.

"No one," Sherman replied. "The person who did this will never be arrested. But he won't get away with it, either."

"Listen, Holmes," the sergeant barked. "I'm not in the mood for riddles."

"There was no murder, sergeant, just an attempt at insurance fraud." Before Wilson could explode, Sherman continued. "Hunter committed suicide—not unexpected, considering his business failure and bad health. But he wanted Doug to collect his insurance. So, he turned on the gas, gave himself a bonk with the bat, then called his son's home number. He didn't call the police or his son's cell phone. Help might have arrived too quickly."

"So the call for help…"

"Ben said the attacker had gone out into the hall. How did he leave this room and get into the hall?"

"Through the door," Wilson said, trying to hold onto his temper. "It's the only way out of the room."

"Correct. So how did the towel get under the doorjamb? It could only have been done by someone in the room: the victim himself."

Death of a Diva

Sergeant Wilson had been half-prepared for Sherman's announcement. "I knew you'd solve this one," he laughed. "It's got something to do with the sequin on her forehead?"

"Correct." Sherman was impressed.

"It's that actress, Diane, the one with the sequins on her costume."

"Not correct." Sherman felt bad for him. "But a good guess. It was Tommy Burton, the theater owner."

Wilson scratched his head. "What does he have to do with sequins?"

"Tommy's the person who brought sequins into her dressing room—when he brought her the costume. The theater is new, so it couldn't have been there from a previous show. My guess is she hated the costume and made her usual threats about pulling out her money. They fought and she got killed.

"After the murder, Tommy took the costume, along with the others, and visited the dressing rooms in the basement. Then he brought back his nephew as a witness and 'discovered' the body."

"You mean it couldn't have been Diane?"

"Afraid not. Diane didn't receive her costume until Tommy gave it to her. From that moment on, she was with other people. No, the only person who could have gotten a red sequin into Leona's dressing room before the murder was Tommy."

About the Author and Illustrator

An Edgar-nominated mystery author, Hy Conrad is a writer and story editor on the television series *Monk*. His previous work includes designing and writing games for Parker Brothers, Hasbro, and Milton Bradley. He has lent his talents to mysteries in every medium from stage plays to interactive video to computer and online fiction. He is also the author of six previous books of mini-mysteries, published in over a dozen countries.

Tatjana Mai-Wyss is a book illustrator who grew up in Swtizerland and has lived all over the United States. She is currently in the process of moving to New Orleans with her husband, cat, and baby girl Louisa. In love with books as long as she can remember, she works in pen and ink, or watercolor and collage, and always carries a pencil.

Index